The Visitor.

the Visitor

ALSO BY MAEVE BRENNAN

The Springs of Affection
Stories of Dublin

The Long-Winded Lady
Notes from The New Yorker

The Rose Garden
Short Stories

Maeve Brennan

the Visitor

COUNTERPOINT
WASHINGTON, D.C.

The original typescript of *The Visitor* may be found in the Sheed and Ward Family Papers, University of Notre Dame Archives, Notre Dame, Indiana, where it is cataloged as item number CSWD 16/02. The editor wishes to thank Mr. Kevin Cawley, Archivist and Curator of Manuscripts, for his help in preparing this book.

Library of Congress Cataloging-in-Publication Data
is available.
Catalog Card Number 00-055495
ISBN 1-58243-083-7

FIRST EDITION

Book design by David Bullen Design

Printed in the United States of America on acid-free paper that meets the American National Standards Institute z39-48 Standard

COUNTERPOINT
P.O. Box 65793
Washington, D.C. 20035-5793

Counterpoint is a member of the Perseus Books Group.

The Visitor

THE MAIL TRAIN rushed along toward Dublin, and all the passengers swayed and nodded with the uneven rhythm of it and kept their eyes fixed firmly in front of them as though the least movement would bring them to the end of their patience. Luggage had been piled hastily out in the corridor, and some people left their seats and stood there, leaning against windows all cloudy with breath and smoke.

Anastasia King rubbed a clear spot in her window and stared out, but in the rushing darkness only a few stray lights were discernible, blurred by the rain. She turned back into the corridor and took out a cigarette.

Around her in the garish yellow trainlight faces were shadowed and withdrawn, indifference heightened by the deafening clatter of the train. The din automatically raised a barrier of hostile irritation to daunt the chummy souls. She was glad of this.

A man spoke to her, standing very close because of the noise, startling her.

"May I borrow a match?"

"Of course."

She frowned nervously. It occurred to her that he might have asked some other person, and she looked along the corridor. He caught the direction of her glance. He smiled a little.

"They all looked half-asleep," he said, "but I saw you look out through the window there."

"I looked out but I didn't see much. It's raining hard and it's very dark."

"It was raining when I left here. That was nearly two years ago." His voice was idle and friendly. "Have you been away long?"

"Oh, yes, a long time. Six years last month."

"That *is* a long time. You haven't been back at all?"

"No."

After a moment she said, "I've been living in Paris, with my mother. We moved there, six years ago."

"I see." He rubbed a place in the window and peered out. "Well, it's raining all right. You know, if I wasn't sure I'd been away I might think I hadn't gone at all. It was exactly like this the day I left."

He continued to stare out and Anastasia looked at her suitcases again.

I might be leaving too, she thought, instead of coming back.

She rocked with the train, her back to the window, and felt once again that she was remembering a long dream.

The future is wearisome too. I can't imagine it now. It's very late in the evening.

Her thoughts went back to Paris; dwindling uncertain pictures formed in her mind. Again she was saying goodbye to her father. There he was in miniature, and she also, in a clear cold miniature room. He turned and faded out through the hotel door that opened inward. He looked a bit like a tortoise, all bent and curving in on himself, carrying his hat in his hand. For the first time she had wanted to say she was sorry, at last to say how sorry she was, but he was already down the corridor and around the corner and gone.

He was alone and sad. Behind her in this tiny hotel room of memory her mother sat in a chair near the window. Her mother's face was soft from crying, her hands were clasped upturned in her lap, and she met her daughter's gaze with a glance of passive recognition and that was all . . .

The man beside her turned suddenly from the window to face her.

"Ah, I'm glad to be back again," he said with a contented sigh. "I suppose you are too. People to visit, places to see. But you'll find a lot of changes too, and so will I, I suppose. Even two years is a long time, these days."

He smiled and she nodded at him and smiled too. He straightened himself and looked at his watch.

"Well, I'll run along and get my stuff together. We'll soon be pulling in. Thanks for the match. Goodbye now."

A few steps away he turned.

"Have a nice holiday now," he yelled above the train noise.

"It isn't a holiday."

"Oh, well." He was uncertain. "Have a good time. Goodbye."

"Goodbye."

Bags were tumbling down from racks and coats were being pulled on. She looked out again into the darkness, but now there was nothing to be seen but the distorted reflection of the excited scene behind her.

"Here we are in Dublin," said an English voice close to her.

Her eyes filled with tears. She bent to her suitcases. Somewhere in her mind a voice was saying clearly, "Ireland is my dwelling place, Dublin is my station."

Then the porter had found her a taxi and was putting her bags in. She thanked him and tipped him and climbed in alongside the luggage.

She put one hand out to balance the smaller bag, which was in danger of falling, and then suddenly they had left the dim taxicab lane and were in the street, and there were many people, ordinary people, not travelers, walking along the rainy streets. The faces looked just as self-intent and serious as the faces in the strange cities she had seen; they seemed no different.

In a moment the windows were blurred with running water and the streets slid by unnamed and unrecognized. The rain fell slantwise on rows and rows of blank-faced houses, over the slate roofs, past their many windows. Anastasia slumped lower into her seat, trying not to recognize the sudden melancholy that was on her. The cabman drove without a word and his silence seemed sullen. She felt rebuffed for no reason.

It seemed too long to her grandmother's house, but she was startled when the car drew up at last, and she looked up apprehensively and saw the familiar door of years ago. The lights were on in the front hall. They had been waiting for her, her grandmother and Katharine. The door opened wide and lighted the steps for the cab driver, who was struggling up to the door with her bags.

She kissed her grandmother hastily, avoiding her eyes. The grandmother did not move from the door of the sitting room. She stood in the doorway, having just got up from the fireside and her reading, and contemplated Anastasia and Anastasia's luggage crowding the hall. She was still the same, with her delicate and ruminative and ladylike face, and her hands clasped formally in front of her. Anastasia thought, She is waiting for me to make some mistake. Katharine stood as ever in the background, anxious and smiling in her big white apron, her scrubbed hands already reaching to help with the luggage, her eyes lively with pleasure and curiosity.

Anastasia said rapidly, "Did he bring all the bags? I was afraid he'd forget one. It's the little one I'm worried about. It's always getting lost, it's so small. He was an idiot, that man. He talked the head off me, all the way from the station, really—"

The grandmother waited for her to finish.

She said, "It is nice to see you again, Anastasia. You are looking well. Isn't she, Katharine?"

Her voice was cool and unemphatic. Hearing it, Anastasia was held to attention.

"Indeed, she looks grand!" Katharine said enthusiastically. "She's a real young lady! I'd never have known her. How old is it you are, now?"

"Twenty-two," said Anastasia. She touched her hair nervously and smiled at them. Her hair was dark and brushed smoothly back from her forehead. Her mouth was stubborn and her eyes were puzzled under faint, flyaway brows. She was anxious to please.

The grandmother finished looking at her.

"Well," she said. "Katharine tells me your room is all ready for you. Would you like to go on up, and take off your coat?"

This was her own room, the room that had been hers since childhood. It was at the back of the house, on the third floor, and its windows overlooked the garden. She stood for a while by the window, and stared down where the garden was. She yielded for a moment to the disappointment that had been spreading coldly over all the homecoming. She tried to grow quiet, leaning against the hard window glass. She thought of her mother, who had been dead only a month, and the glass became hot with her forehead, and she pressed her hands to her face and tried to forget where she was, and that she was alone in her home.

Home is a place in the mind. When it is empty, it frets. It is fretful with memory, faces and places and times gone by. Beloved images rise up in disobedience and make a mirror for emptiness. Then what resentful wonder, and what half-aimless seeking. It is a silly state of affairs. It is a silly creature that tries to get a smile from even the most familiar and loving shadow. Comical and hopeless, the long gaze back is always turned inward.

The mother's face, intent and gentle, is closer than the rest. Now it is a dead face, with no more bewilderment in it. She used to walk alone in the garden every evening after dinner. Close the eyes to see her again, a solitary figure in the fading light, wandering slowly down the garden and slowly back, between the neat black flowerbeds. It is unbearable to remember.

That was a time of uncertain mood, that time when she used to walk in the garden. Then the family, the sparse little family, was together, the grandmother, the father, the mother, the child. They were together and it was no satisfaction to them.

At night after supper they gathered together around the living-room fire and then quite soon separated, and went to their own rooms. While Anastasia was small she went the first. Taking her mother's hand she proceeded upstairs and was put to bed. Her room was papered with pink and blue rosebuds in fancy baskets and she was in the habit of watching one of the baskets until she fell asleep. Her mother would fuss quietly about, tidying things away, arranging clothes, straightening up. Often Anastasia roused from sleep to see her mother sitting motionless at the window, looking out at the darkness. She would speak to her.

"Mother."

"Yes, pet. Go back to sleep."

"What's out there, mother?"

"The garden, silly."

"It's dark in the garden now, isn't it?"

"Yes. Very dark. You ought to be asleep."

"What time is it?"

"It's terribly late. It's nine-thirty, and time for you to shut up both eyes and go fast asleep. Fast asleep, now."

Fast asleep. Once the mother came and crept into Anastasia's bed at night.

She said, "I'm cold, pet, and you're warm as toast always."

The bed was too narrow for the two of them. After a while they fell asleep.

At breakfast time Anastasia said proudly to her father, "Mother says I'm warm as toast."

He laughed at her.

"I'm sure you are, at that."

"She came and got into bed with me last night. She was cold and I warmed her up."

The father looked up in surprise.

The mother said, "You're a great talker, Anastasia."

"Why on earth was that necessary, Mary?"

"Ah, John, don't be angry. I was only cold."

"I'm not angry, for God's sake. Haven't you enough blankets on your bed without disturbing the child in the middle of the night?"

"Ah, I was lonely, that's all."

She began to cry, stirring her tea.

The father said, "Anastasia, go away and play like a good girl."

The grandmother, Mrs. King, came in, prayer book in hand from early mass.

"What's this?" she said. "What's this now?"

She said, "John, tell me what's up. Why is Mary crying?"

"It's nothing, mother."

She sat down at the head of the table, facing her son, and poured tea for herself.

"This is ridiculous," she said, "scenes at breakfast. It's something I'm not accustomed to in this house."

The mother looked up with a wet trembling face. She looked back then in desperation at the tea she was stirring.

"I'm not accustomed to them either. I'm not accustomed to them either. You needn't belittle me." Her voice shook, and her mouth lifted nervously into an imitation smile.

"Great God," said the father. "You'll drive me mad."

"Mary," said the grandmother, smiling, "you're making a fool of yourself."

"You're trying to belittle me," said the mother in a disappearing voice. "In front of the child. That's what you're after, to turn her against me too."

The father threw his cigarette on the floor.

The grandmother looked at him.

"What brought all this on anyway?" she asked pleasantly.

She began to butter her toast. One hand held the toast firm. The other spread a neat layer of butter. Anastasia's mouth watered, although she had just finished breakfast. The grandmother stretched across the table to her.

"Here, pet," she said, "have this nice toast."

"It's nothing at all," said the father. "Only a stupid argument. Mary hasn't enough blankets, and she had to sleep with Anastasia last night, she was so cold."

"Is that true, Mary? You know you can have all the blankets you want. All you have to do is tell me."

The mother folded her napkin and stood up. She was no longer crying.

She said, "It's all right."

"What's all right?" asked the father. "Why don't you come right out with it, whatever it is?"

She said again, "It's all right," and she pushed her chair tidily into place and went out of the room.

"Poor child," said the grandmother conversationally. "She's too intense altogether. She takes things to heart."

"She does that," said the father. "I never know how to take her. I never know what to say. Whatever I say is wrong."

"That's the way it is with some people," said the grandmother. "Don't blame her. It's the way she was brought up."

Anastasia finished her toast and waited for a nod from her grandmother. She wanted a smile of approval. She wanted to be seen. But they were busy with politics, and after a few restless minutes she slipped down from her chair and away without being noticed.

The trees around Noon Square grew larger, as daylight faded. Darkness stole out of the thickening trees and slurred the thin iron railings around the houses, and spread quickly across the front gardens, making the grass go black and taking the color from the flowers. The darkness of night fell on the green park in the middle of the square, and rose fast to envelop the tall patient houses all around. The street lamps drew flat circles of light around them and settled down for the night.

All the houses in the square were tall, with heavy stone steps going up to the front doors. They were occupied by old people, who had grown old in their houses and their accustomed ways. They disregarded the inconveniences of the square houses, their dark basements and drafty landings, and lived on, going tremulously from one wrinkled day to the next, with an occasional walk between the high stone walls of their gardens.

It was November when Anastasia came home from Paris. She sat in the living room, across the fire from her grandmother. It was an enormous shadowy room, and for light they had only the fire and one lamp. The fire was hot and bright. It threw trembling light to the farthest corner of the room, and hesitated across the old dull pattern of the wallpaper. There was no movement in the room except the wild movement of the fire-flames and the light they let go. The light washed up and down the room like thin water over stones.

Anastasia looked suddenly up at the mirror that hung over the mantel. It did not lie flat against the wall, but hung out slightly at the top. It reflected the fringed hearthrug where she had played when she was a little child, hearing the conversation go to and fro over her head. She looked hard at it, thinking that somewhere in its depths it must retain a faint image of the faces it had reflected.

She had often looked up and seen her father and mother stirring there, faces half in shadow and half in light, and sometimes one of them had looked up and found her watching. During these evenings it had been her habit to steal away from the fire and hide herself behind the heavy window curtains, wrapping herself in their musty voluminous depth, so that the room sounds were muffled and only the silent, dimly lighted square below was real, and that not too real, with its infrequent lamps, its brooding trees, and the shrouded passersby.

Standing behind the curtain she would launch herself into a world of dreams; she would deliberately absorb herself in a long, long dream, which would suddenly end and start all over again before the moment of discovery and the safe journey home to bed.

She rose abstractedly and crossed the room and twitched the curtains apart. There was no one standing behind the curtains. The square below was the same. The lamps were no brighter than she remembered, and the trees seemed the same. A lonely figure went along in the darkness as she watched.

She turned and looked at the mirror, but it reflected only empty chairs, and the firelight played indifferently on polished furniture as it had once across her parents' faces. There is the background, and it is exactly the same. She let the curtains fall back into place and went back to her chair.

Her grandmother roused and put aside her book and took off her spectacles and sat moving them in her hand.

She said, "How long do you intend to stay here, Anastasia?"

Anastasia shrank in surprise.

"Well, indefinitely, Grandmother."

After a time, into the silence, she said lamely, "Why, Grandmother? I'm afraid I didn't consider doing anything else, except coming here. After she died, I came straightaway, as soon as I could settle things. She wanted me to."

"Did she?"

Mrs. King said in her gentle voice, "You know, Anastasia, you made a serious choice when you decided to stay with your mother in Paris. You were sixteen then, not a child. You knew what she had done. You were aware of the effect it was having on your father."

She turned the spectacles thoughtfully in her hands.

"Didn't you know what state he was in, when he left you in Paris, after trying to get you to come back here, and had to come alone?"

"Oh, Grandmother," cried Anastasia, "how could I leave her?"

"We won't go into that. I am going to be very matter-of-fact with you, Anastasia."

Her voice was very matter-of-fact.

"You know that your mother disgraced us all, running off the way she did, like some kind of a madwoman."

She said, half-amused, "Did you know that she went to one of the clerks in your father's office, begging money for her ticket?"

Anastasia stood up in great agitation.

"She hardly knew what she was doing, Grandma. You should have seen her when I saw her, in Paris that time. She was half out of her mind."

She began to cry, helplessly and awkwardly.

"She is dead, the Lord have mercy on her," said Mrs. King cautiously. "I'll speak no ill of her. Don't cry, Anastasia, I didn't mean to hurt your feelings."

She glanced toward the window.

"What did she go to Paris for, of all places? Will you tell me that?"

Remember that sad elderly pilgrimage, made long before its time, to a strange French address. They found the street with difficulty, and then the house, but no one there remembered the name they mentioned. Anastasia tried automatically to recall the address, and frowning, caught her grandmother watching her.

She said without interest, "I'm not sure what she wanted. She didn't know herself. She was looking for someone she remembered from when she was at school there, but they had moved away. It was just an idea she had."

Mrs. King drew back and sighed.

"Ah, I suppose it was a pitiful case, at that."

She was silent, reviewing something bitter in her mind.

She said at last, "A pity she sent for you, Anastasia, and a pity you went after her. It broke your father's heart."

Anastasia said nothing. She felt tired, and sat down where she stood, on the hearthrug.

"Well, it's a good thing that you came home, even if only for a visit. Your father would be glad to know that you are here, God rest his soul."

The grandmother got up and collected her things from the table beside her. Her movements were stiff but determined. She always moved as though she knew exactly what she was doing.

"Are you ready for bed now, child?"

"Not yet, Grandma. I'll stay by the fire a while."

She looked up timidly.

"Grandma, what did you mean just now, 'only for a visit'? I was really hoping to stay here for good."

Mrs. King turned to her.

"No, Anastasia. That's out of the question. You kept the flat there, didn't you?"

"Yes. I was in a hurry to get away. I thought I'd go back later and clear things up."

"I'm afraid you've been counting too much on me. You mustn't do that. I have no home to offer you. This is a changed house here now. I see no one whatsoever."

She smiled with anger.

"I stopped seeing them after she ran off, when I found them

asking questions of Katharine in the hall outside. I go out to mass, that's all. When I got your telegram, I hadn't the heart to stop you. You need a change. It's natural that you should want to pay a visit here. But more than that, no. It might have been different, maybe, if you'd been with me when he died. But you weren't here."

There was no comfort in her. Anastasia gazed at her, and afterward gazed at the place where she had been standing. She watched the leaping flames till they began to die down. The red bars of the grate turned to gray and then to rusty black. There was an occasional weak flicker in the fading coals. She dozed, sitting on the rug. Shortly after midnight a light rain fell again, spit down the chimney and knocked a sizzle out of the dead fire. The little sound disturbed her and she sat up drowsily, chilled by the passing of a cold breeze that blew down the chimney and skittered soundlessly about the room. The silent dark room frightened her and she stumbled to the doorway. But the light in the hall reassured her, and so did the steady rise and fall of her grandmother's breathing as she passed the open bedroom door on the second floor.

Anastasia slept heavily through the rest of the night, while the rain fell down outside. Some people in the city half wakened and listened for a while to the steady drumming on their dripping windowsills. Underneath the street lamps the circles of light were changed to shining pools of darkness and made crooked mirrors for faraway stars. All the clocks tolled the hours slowly, till the first spreading light of day came to show a gray morning, inside the house and out.

Always, through the winter months, the house and garden remained apart, as though they had been separated from each other. It had been like that since earliest memory. The low stone walls closed in tight around the empty flowerbeds and the patch of grass, now frozen hard, or soggy after rain. The wooden seat near the laburnum tree never dried enough to sit on. If one looked from the house the garden seemed enclosed in hard silence. And yet if by chance one walked to the end of the garden and turned to see, then the house itself had a withdrawn look, a severe incurious aspect. Standing outside in the wintertime one was cut off and left, because the green life in the earth around was discouraged now, or secret, and in any case offered no welcome.

In the kitchen the big oven was kept going from morning till night, and it filled the basement with great comfortable heat. On the worst winter days, and on other days, Katharine brought poor men in to sit at her table and gave them a meal. A lot of poor men and poor women came asking at the basement door. Sometimes they sang outside first, with quick eyes searching the upper windows; or they carefully unwrapped a tin whistle or a violin and played for a while; or they sold shoelaces and pencils; but they were all poor people.

("Don't ever say beggar," said Katharine to Anastasia in a fierce whisper. "He's a poor man, God help him.")

People seldom went through the back door that led from the garden into the narrow alley behind the house in wintertime, because the way grew caked with leaves then, and slushy. Errand boys on bicycles used it as a shortcut. They slithered up and down at high speed. They whistled as they went and greeted each other in loud voices.

All the long-ago winters seemed to have disappeared in firelight. In memory the silent flames played gently from all the small grates in the house, warming the hands and faces of the family. There was Katharine, bending herself down to poke at a stubborn log. And the mother, that pale and most unluxurious person, drawing close to the heat after a walk outside.

With the coming of spring, windows were thrown wide all over the house, and the garden seemed to smile with the new colors in it. The cat waited impatiently for her breakfast on the cement outside the kitchen door, instead of huddling by the warm stove as she did in the cold weather. In the early spring and summer mornings the sun lay clean across the cement outside the door there, and the cat laid her ears back and made the milk fly. There were little creeping insects that came out of the wall to walk in the sun, but Katharine's broom made short work of them.

Plants were taken out of their pots and planted into the earth, and the red flowerpots were put away till next winter.

Next winter and next winter and next winter. In the mind they passed all slowly, like clouds across a summer sky, but a sudden call or turn of the head and they disappeared in a rush, shuttling quickly one after the last till nothing was left but a strangeness in the mind, a drop of thought that trembled a moment and was gone, perhaps.

Anastasia walked in the park, in front of the house. She walked along the edge path as far as she could go, until she had walked around the whole park twice. Then she changed her direction and went straight into the not mysterious middle of the park, where she found, as she expected, a small stone house, a summer house that contained two long stone benches where nursemaids had been apt to sit in the sunny weather. She went in and sat down.

The summer house was open on all sides, and from where she sat she could see her grandmother's house. She could feel the silence of it, and she stared at it. This raw cold day the park had been deserted since morning, and now evening was closing quickly in, closing down on the city. She sat there in the cold.

Someone came hurrying around the corner and went straight to the house as she watched. Who could it be? It was a woman and she wore a hat and beyond that there was nothing to remark about her. She had a hand at the doorbell, and Anastasia watching felt the sudden ringing through the house. How astonished they must be. She knew how it sounded. Sudden and loud in the kitchen, where Katharine would at this moment be gathering herself in annoyed surprise for the climb to the hall. Distant and sweet in her grandmother's room, still more distant in her own room.

I doubt if that bell has rung since I rang it myself the first night home, five weeks ago.

Then she remembered how the door had opened while she was still in the taxicab. That night there had been no necessity to ring the bell at all. Now Katharine opened the door and the visitor stepped in. She stepped into the hall and the door closed on their faces, turned to each other. Immediately the light went on in the sitting room and there they were again, vaguely. Katharine came to the window and drew the curtains. She had her head turned, talking behind her. The light went on in Mrs. King's room. She has roused from her nap, and is coming down. Anastasia pictured her grandmother sitting on the edge of her large bed, touching her hair, fastening the collar at her throat, staring a moment at the floor before starting stiffly into the evening's activity: tea and the fireside, dinner and the fireside.

Someone came out on the steps. It was Katharine in her big white apron. She waved vigorously at Anastasia. Probably she is smiling. Even if she can't see me, she knows I'm here. She's been watching all the time, thought Anastasia, and she looked up high above the roof of the house, up to the deepening sky, to shut out Katharine and her wave and the open door. When she looked again, warily, Katharine was still there, still waving, and the visitor had come to the window and was standing between the curtains looking out.

Anastasia looked at Katharine, waving on the steps. She searched for the spot where Katharine's eyes, now frowning, might be. She looked straight at Katharine's eyes and gave no sign at all that she saw her. She did not move. Katharine turned and went into the house and shut the door behind her. In the sitting-room window the curtains fell to. Now she could see the darkness. There were the lonely lights of the street lamps, and a faint gray haze in the air, left over from daytime. That will soon disappear, and the stars will be out full. Not yet a while.

She got up and walked toward the house, back across the park. It was teatime and a little after. She entered the house by a side door and went silently up to her room. Sometime later Katharine tapped on the door. She came in smiling. There was no ill temper in her face. She looked tired and pleasant.

"Your grandmother says will you come down and have a cup of tea with herself and Miss Kilbride. Miss Kilbride wants to see you particularly. You'll remember her. She's the only one comes now at all."

"Oh, I do remember her, very well. My mother was very fond of her. Of course I remember."

She went to the mirror.

She said, "Nobody comes at all, do they?"

Katharine looked at her with a distant considering eye.

"No one much comes, no. Did you have a nice walk? I tried to catch you earlier, to get you in, but you weren't looking. Well, do you want your tea? I put on an extra cup for you."

"I'm coming."

She went down. The grandmother was in her usual place in

her own chair. Facing her was a small wrinkled woman with faded green eyes and astonishing coal black hair, which she wore parted in the middle and drawn into a bun low on her neck. She was smoking, holding the cigarette delicately as though it might explode in her face. She held the cigarette to one side and looked carefully at Anastasia's legs, and then she looked at her face and smiled affably and held out her hand.

"My dear, dear child," she said. "Do you remember me at all?"

She had a breathless voice, and she coughed gently.

Anastasia smiled warmly at her. She was glad she had come down. She glanced at her grandmother, who apparently was admiring the teacups. Katharine came in with hot water and a plate of scones. Katharine hoped the tea was strong enough.

Anastasia thought, She's always carrying a tray or something. She's always been carrying things in and out through doorways, and then she must know a lot too. She must think to herself a great deal.

Katharine straightened up from the tea tray.

She said, "My sister was telling me a terrible thing. About a mother of a friend of hers who was killed by a train the other day. No. The train didn't really kill her. She wandered away from them, out of the house one night. A humor took her, she went down on the tracks. She got past the tracks all right, and then she fell down. It was the sight and noise of the big engine so close, I suppose. She got up later and talked all right, but she died the next day."

She looked at them all with a frightened inquiring glance. They were silent to her.

Anastasia said, "Poor old woman."

Mrs. King said, "Her time had *come,* Katharine."

"Will there be anything else?" asked Katharine, and she went out of the room and shut the door quietly behind her.

They all sat there with their tea. Miss Kilbride sat in her chair, not relaxed. She paid attention to everything; even a sudden spurt from the fire drew a little smile from her. Her eyes went constantly to Anastasia's face, and Anastasia knew of this scrutiny, and the grandmother knew of it too, and was no longer amused by it, but uncomfortable and cross because of it. Her crossness showed in the abrupt way she handled the teacups. She was irritated at the sudden life that moved in the room, seeing curiosity and conjecture where for so long there had been only unaltering melancholy and lengthening memories. Yet she was complacent, being removed from the shy conversational strivings that marked the renewing of acquaintance between Anastasia and Miss Norah Kilbride. They were lonely and unsatisfied, and she was lonely and satisfied and closed.

At six o'clock Miss Kilbride got up and put on her hat, a little round hat that looked like a man's bowler, with a curling feather at the side. She peered into the mirror and patted her hair. She said goodbye, and, smiling and nodding, made Anastasia promise to visit her soon.

"She is mad as a hatter," said the grandmother cheerfully, after she had gone. "She is my oldest friend, but I think she's mad. That's a wig she wears."

"Is she bald?"

"I think she is, or nearly so, anyway. She had an illness years ago, and her health never really returned to her. That was when she began to lose her hair. She used to have rather fair brown hair. She had a demon of a mother, who was bedridden but ruled her house with a rod of iron. She managed to stop Norah from marrying, too. She's thirty years dead, and she still has that girl under her thumb."

Anastasia sat on the edge of her chair and looked into the fire. The grandmother sighed.

"Listen to me," she said, "calling her a girl. She's over seventy and younger than I am myself at that. We two were at school together. Poor Norah. I think she likes her wig, though."

Anastasia smiled over at her.

"She pats it as if she were fond of it," she said.

"You ought to go see her soon," said Mrs. King. "She's a poor lonely thing."

After a time the Christmas season came. Anastasia found a great deal of pleasure in buying presents for her grandmother and for Katharine. She wrapped them in ceremonial paper, in secret, and hid them in a low drawer in her wardrobe. She spent every afternoon in the shops. She found herself walking down Grafton

Street. The crowd surrounded her with noise and hurry, the Christmas crowd, inattentive, preoccupied with lists and plans, while she, without pressing business, kept her mind with her and took notice of small things that interested her. She listened to the excited voices of the children and watched their mothers, those with money and those with little to spare.

In one large shop on Grafton Street she stood irresolute and watched two girls choose a necklace. They looked up and saw her, and she pretended to be watching for someone. People were coming into the shop, and she watched from where she stood and found after a time that she was looking intently for her mother's face.

Then it seemed that her mother entered, wearing the familiar small black hat, and walked toward the staircase with precise busy steps. Her face was serene, and her eyes held the clear look she wore for strangers.

I can see her back, even. And she watched the slender upright back disappear up the stairs.

She thought, She has gone to the dress department, and without hesitation she hurried herself to the dress department.

"Have you seen my mother?" she asked one of the girls. "She's not very tall, wearing a black coat and a small hat with a bird on it. She was just here, I think."

"We've been busy, Miss," said the girl. "I noticed no one in particular."

Well, I can't leave her here, thought Anastasia. She wandered idly about for a few minutes but could not bring her mother's face to mind.

She left the shop and went into a church nearby, where she lighted a candle and knelt to pray. After a time she saw her mother slip into a place a few seats ahead of her. There she knelt motionless as she always knelt, with her face upturned to the altar. Her hands were gathered in front of her, holding her rosary.

I can leave her here—and she stepped reluctantly out into the aisle and genuflected. Happy Christmas, she whispered as she bent her knee, and she made her way slowly to the back of the church. She slipped an offering into the poor box and blessed herself with holy water. She was trembling, and in that soft uncertain grateful mood that easily gives way to tears. It was already dark, but the air in the street seemed to shine after the heavy darkness of the chapel.

In the hall at home Katharine came smiling to greet her. She was tying her apron behind her back.

"Your grandmother wanted a word with you when you came in. She's at her tea. You look perished with the cold, child."

"I am a bit cold."

She threw her coat across the hall chair. She looked into the hall mirror and smoothed her hair. The grandmother was waiting for her. Her white hair lifted lightly away from her forehead, from her cool old blue eyes.

"Had you a nice walk, Anastasia?"

at that grassy place in Stephen's Green (where we always went after mass) or even in fingering books outside the old corner shop on the quays. One goes to stand alone on a city bridge, to look over at the water, and suddenly one's eyes are sliding from right to left, from left to right, to see if some person is watching, some stranger who thinks it odd to stand alone, looking over the bridge with nothing to do. One must be about one's business. There is no patience for solitary aimless wistful hangers-on who want to sit and watch, or who ludicrously join the crowd in its rush to the end of the street, and then pause at the corner, confused, directionless, stupid.

Even in a shop, when one sits down for a lemonade, there comes the moment to stand up and pay the cashier and go out on the street again and start walking again. One is bound to be sent scurrying back to the place one came from, which is the other world, the first world, the one with walls around it.

This is quite different. It is a standstill. There is silence upstairs and downstairs, behind the closed doors and in the hall and on the landings. There is no compulsion at all. The slow-turning malicious sightless eye of the crowd is not here. One can spend hour upon hour here, watching through the window the changing sky, or reading books, papers, and magazines, or even sleeping. Inside the house there is no further step to be taken, except perhaps to find a coat and gloves, and go out again onto the street.

It was late February, and frosty weather.

Anastasia came slowly in from the street and closed the front door behind her. She loosened her coat and took off her gloves. At the foot of the stairs the crackle and bang of the newly lighted fire caught her ear and drew her to the sitting-room door. She leaned against the door frame and gazed absently into the room, shrugging her shoulders a little to throw off the chill that clung to her. The dark masses of the room loomed toward her, soft gloom broken briefly by the sputtering fire, and again twice by the large rectangular windows, through which the square could be seen lying like a pale stage backdrop, out there beyond.

She heard Katharine begin her ascent of the stairs from the kitchen, climbing heavily from step to step, carrying the heavy tea tray. Katharine is kind, but she is inquisitive and officious. She owns the place.

Over by the fireplace the first warm waves began to circle out. She went to lean against the mantelpiece and felt the heat on her legs. There in the mirror was Katharine, easing the heavy curtains over so that they joined together and shut out the square and the pale evening sky. The twilight was gone, shut out of the room. There was only the fire left to turn to. It threw noisy sparks up into the chimney and out onto the hearthrug, while at its center it burned away forever without end.

One lamp was switched on and Katharine stood in the middle of the room.

"I can see you in the mirror, Katharine." All teasingly.

"Indeed you can, I know that well." Katharine gave her an odd look, half-startled.

She thinks I'm a queer one, thought Anastasia indifferently. Mrs. King came into the room in silence. She sat down without speaking, arranging her long black skirt about her long-hidden, unimaginable knees, and examining the tea tray with a critical eye. Katharine peered into the teapot and assured herself that the tea was ready. She went away.

Mrs. King glanced up at Anastasia.

"It's nice to see you down to tea for a change, child. Why don't you sit down and be comfortable?"

She filled the cups. They added sugar and cream. Anastasia added a little more sugar. The room was very still again, except for the large disturbing movement of the firelight. Once or twice Mrs. King stirred uneasily and glanced across the hearth at her granddaughter. There was impatience and distress on her face.

Anastasia thought, As usual I'm being a strain on her. She stood up and put down her cup.

"Excuse me, Grandma. I have a bit of reading to do."

"Anastasia. Wait a minute. I want to have a word with you."

She put aside her teacup.

"Look here, Anastasia," she said decisively. "What plans have you made for yourself?"

"I haven't made any plans."

Mrs. King sighed with irritation.

"Don't you think it's about time you did make some plans?"

"Why? I want to stay here."

The grandmother raised her hands and dropped them helplessly.

"You are trying to drive me mad," she said distinctly. "I wish to God, and wish this every day of my life, that you would go away and leave me alone here. You cry, you're forever opening a door and coming into the room where I happen to be at the moment, and so on and on—"

"I don't mean it."

"You're not happy here, that's plain. It is really better all around if you go back to Paris as soon as possible."

"What would I do there?" asked Anastasia weakly.

"At your age there are many things you can find to do. You must have friends there. You can stay with the nuns till you get settled somewhere, if you don't want to go back to the flat you shared with your mother (God rest her). As a matter of fact, it might not be quite suitable for you to live alone there. There's that to think of. And you can find some work perhaps, teaching in a school. You might like library work. Have you thought of that?"

"Oh, I have no training, you know that."

"Never mind about that. I have written to the Mother Superior already. She is delighted to have you as assistant in the library, and you can live at the school with the other teachers."

Anastasia had retreated across a wide distance in her mind.

She said unevenly, "Whatever I do, I won't live at the convent. I can work in a library here. I'll take a room and stay in Dublin."

"I control your allowance, Anastasia, and I know what's best for you."

She got up suddenly.

"I'll arrange about money, and so on," she said in a low voice.

She walked rapidly and nervously out of the room. After a moment Anastasia followed her, gathering her coat and gloves as she passed through the hall. Upstairs in her room she closed the window and began to change her dress. With her belt unfastened and hanging loosely she walked over to the window and looked out.

In the late-evening light the garden seemed unreal, a careless impression of a garden with all the colors running into one another. On the end wall was a blurred yellow smudge. That would be the early forsythia. The laburnum tree spread crooked brown arms over the low stone wall. Later it would be a fragrant yellow cloud, shedding its little shining flowers with every ripple of the air. There was a woodshed down there too, almost out of sight from the window, it was so close to the house. It had a slanting corrugated tin roof, and on wet days the rain hammered thunderously down on the roof, filling the interior of the shed with mad imperious sound, so that sometimes a little child playing there would suddenly become terrified, and would run to the kitchen door and enter in breathless haste, to find the sound still persisting, but more remote now, and not so urgent.

This was the shadowy twilight time, when at a little distance familiar things seemed half-strange, when the face of the city seemed averted and almost hidden in the low sky, and drifting clouds came down and fumbled in the outlying hills, to the confusion of the watcher. Anastasia stared listlessly in the direction of the hills, and she fancied she glimpsed them.

That night she had a vivid dream. She dreamed that on a walk down Noon Square she stopped to look behind her, and on turning again to go on her way she found herself tangled in a gardenia bush, which grew up against the window of a big old house. The bush was covered with flowers, creamy white, large and perfect. She stayed to admire them and noticed with a start a wrinkled, purplish old hand that fumbled against the inside of the window without knocking.

A maid came to the door, an old woman, and told her to go away. Anastasia said, with friendly dignity, in her dream, "I am waiting for someone, and as I dropped a piece of paper here, I thought I would wait here."

But the owner of the wrinkled hand, who was the mistress of the house, came out, and with her came her two aged sisters, and they all stood together on the steps of the house. They were all old, with thin, hostile faces, and they told Anastasia to go away, without listening to her friendly dignified speech.

Whereupon she lost her temper and called loudly to the oldest one, "You are a hateful bloody old bitch."

She woke excited with the words in her mouth. Katharine was knocking at the door, and calling her sharply.

"Oh, come on in, Katharine," she cried impatiently. "What is it?"

Katharine came in, weeping.

"Miss Kilbride is dead, the Lord have mercy on her."

She went to close the window.

"We just got word. The maid found her this morning when she went in with a cup of tea to her. She must have died during the night, all alone there, not a soul near. They're burying her on Friday."

Anastasia threw back the bedclothes and pulled on a dressing gown. She sank down on the bed and stared at the floor.

She said, "It's all very sad."

She felt nothing but a suffocating impatience with Katharine. She wished that Katharine would go away and leave her alone.

"There's a letter she left for you," said Katharine, curiosity lending new life to her voice.

It was addressed in Miss Kilbride's handwriting, which Anastasia had never seen before. *Miss A. King. Deliver at once. Dear Anastasia, dear child, do not forget me. God bless you. Norah K.*

Katharine stood close and Anastasia handed the note to her.

"Read it if you like," she said indifferently. "It's about some masses she asked me to have said for her, in case of her death."

"A word from the dead," said Katharine, and she read it reverently and handed it back. Anastasia folded it and laid it away on the table and stared at it with heavy eyes.

"You know, Katharine," she said. "I'll be leaving soon. My grandmother wants me to go back to Paris."

"Well, now, child," said Katharine in a soothing voice. "Maybe it's for the best. Sure, this is no sort of a house for a young girl to be living in, with two old women like your grandmother and me."

"I don't know why you're all so anxious to get rid of me," cried Anastasia, between tears and anger. "This is my home. I don't know what harm I'm doing you all, that you object to me so."

Katharine sat down confidentially on the edge of the bed beside Anastasia.

"Your grandmother is doing what she thinks is best for you, child. You know she wouldn't want to hurt you."

Anastasia gave her a look, and got to her feet. She crossed to the dressing table and began to brush her hair.

"Well, there's no sense talking about it. I have to go, that's plain enough. And you seem to agree with her, so what chance do I have?

"You'd better get along down to her, Katharine. She's probably upset by all this. And take the note. She'll be wanting to see what's in it."

Katharine looked at her helplessly and went out. She stuck her head back into the room.

"Your breakfast will be ready when you are. Your grandmother will be going over to the house this afternoon. Will I tell her you'll go with her? Miss Kilbride was very fond of you."

"No." Anastasia turned on her. "I won't go over there. I couldn't bear it. Don't tell her I'll go."

Katharine was shocked.

"You can talk to her about it yourself, downstairs," she said, in deep disapproval, and closed the door.

After she had gone, Anastasia took the envelope Miss Kilbride's letter had come in and tore it into little bits. She dressed quickly, found her purse, and left the house without seeing anyone. The thought of her dream of the gardenias returned to her. I think too much about myself, she thought. I think too much about myself. But this idea did not really worry her, for she felt cut off from all the other people in the street around, and more isolated than they.

It was about nine o'clock in the morning, a fine sunless day. People were going to work. She took a bus to a place outside the city, near an old water-filled quarry that was said to be bottomless. She had to walk a way from the bus to get there, but the way was familiar to her. She found that she knew every turn of the road. Some landmarks came sooner than she expected, and some she had entirely forgotten but recognized at once on seeing them. It seemed as though, if she took the time, she could recall some story about every tree along the way. Her mind was disturbed with indistinct memories, but she continued walking and made her way along—it was a rough countryside road, hardly more than a lane—without attempting to trace back any of the thoughts that started up within her. Coming at last to the quarry, she felt as though she had passed through a crowd of old friends, without having paused to call one name to mind.

She went to the very edge, walking cautiously over the stony waste ground that surrounded it. It was the story that a stone dropped there would never stop falling. Little boys playing liked to test the story, throwing stones in there, time and time again. They would hurl with all the strength of their weedy little arms and listen fearfully for the distant sound that should come when the stone hit bottom. There was never any sound, no sound whatever, and only the quiet looping ripples to satisfy them that they had done any throwing at all.

Anastasia took Miss Kilbride's wedding ring from her purse. It was still wrapped in tissue paper, a tiny package. She tossed it into the water. It made no sound, going. She hardly knew that it had left her hand. There it would fall forever with the falling stones, past and to come. She backed away from the edge and stood a moment abstracted in a stare. Poor little Other Self, she thought, and contemplated the cold thankless water, which shook a little in the wind.

The look of the water was unpleasant, and she left it, walking quietly back to the bus along the quiet hedgebound country road. Occasionally she saw a house, sitting well back in its own land, but there was not a soul in sight. How peaceful it was that morning, without sun or sound.

She thought of her grandmother, entering Miss Kilbride's house, viewing the body of her friend. She was glad not to be there, pressing through their common grief to smell the new grave flowers. She was glad to be rid of the wedding ring. Yet now her hasty morning bravado deserted her, and she was tormented with flabby disgust of herself and her cowardice, which sucked away at her will and left her weak and bent with humiliation. She gazed upward at the sky in a childish gesture of question. Then she remembered that her decision had been made for her, and the flat in Paris rushed at her, and the thought of her mother's thin face pinched her heart, and she bowed her head in sickness of memory. The days ahead stretched back to a delirium of loneliness. What to do? What to do? There is no choice, she thought, nodding her head ruefully.

She got up on the bus and paid her fare mechanically. She was being carried back through a stretch of gentle listless countryside, neat fields and hedges and solitary houses with gardens beside them. A quick sentimental sadness touched her, warming her like a soft and familiar coat, sweetening the unhappiness, sweetening it.

It occurred to her, suddenly, that her grandmother might have changed her mind. With Miss Kilbride's death and all, things might be different. This seemed reasonable, even probable. There was almost no doubt about it. She hurried.

The house was empty. They were over at Miss Kilbride's. She lighted the fire in the sitting room and sat down beside it to wait, and yawned at the clock. It was exactly noon. The room grew more and more silent. There was the distant ringing that lies at the end of long deep silence, so that one listens, and slips from listening into reverie, and thence by degrees to some place where the mind has no anchor, and the heart ceases to complain, and beats privately back and backward, toward some endlessly distant and gentle beginning . . .

Their voices clattered loudly into her sleep. The grandmother advanced across the floor and Katharine crowded behind her. She jumped up and confronted them with a timid smile of welcome. Their faces were depressed and cross. Even Katharine seemed abstracted, as she took Mrs. King's hat and then her coat. She shook the coat out and laid it over her arm, and thoughtfully stuck the long hatpins side by side into the band of the hat.

"I'll get you a cup of tea, ma'am," she said with doleful matter-of-factness, and went out at once. Mrs. King sat stiffly down in her chair and glanced at Anastasia.

"Well. So now you won't even go pay your respects to our dead friend, God rest her. Our only friend, who would have given her right arm to help any one of us."

"I couldn't go, Grandma. I didn't think you'd mind."

She met a smile of irritation.

"The number of times I've heard your mother say just that. 'I didn't think you'd mind.' "

She changed the subject with a change in her voice. "To get

back to our conversation of last night, Anastasia. About your going. I've asked Katharine to get out your suitcases. I've written to the bank about money arrangements. And I've written to the Mother Superior at the convent to expect a visit from you in the near future. If you don't want to go to a hotel, you can stay with them till you get the flat opened. I have also written to a Mrs. Drumm, a very old friend of mine, to keep an eye on you. She has your address and so on. I suppose you have all the keys."

"Yes, I have them," said Anastasia hopelessly.

"Don't look at me as though you were being condemned to death, child. The sooner you get this over with, the better for all of us."

She gazed at her with impatient pity and annoyance.

Anastasia stammered, "You really do want to be rid of me, don't you?"

"Oh, now, now, now."

She plucked nervously at her long skirt and stood up. Katharine came in with the tea. Mrs. King spoke sharply to her.

"I'll drink it upstairs in my room, Katharine. I'd like to lie down for an hour."

Katharine glanced at them with alarmed curiosity and backed out.

"Oh, Grandma, Grandma, I'm the only one you have. I don't want to go."

"We can do without that, Anastasia."

Anastasia found herself looking at the shut door. Her hands

held each other in a strong and comfortless grip, and they had grown large.

"Shame on you!" she called out loudly. "Oh, shame on you!"

There was a suitcase flat on the floor under the wardrobe in her room and she rushed upstairs and pulled it out and began to lift things into it.

Katharine came to the door and went away. At once Mrs. King came, shutting the door behind her and looked concernedly about.

"Katharine told me you were packing to go," she said. "There's no need for this. There's no need for all this rush, Anastasia. Now take your time and come and have something to eat. Let the packing wait till tomorrow. Come, now, Anastasia, speak to your grandmother."

Anastasia straightened from packing and looked at her.

"Ah, yes," she said absently. "Off I go."

Mrs. King looked distraught. She picked up a pair of gloves lying in an open drawer of the dressing table and looked at them. She took the photograph of the father from the dressing table and surveyed it.

"This was taken in his last year at university," she said mournfully, with an eye on Anastasia.

"I have to leave," said Anastasia. "It might as well be now."

"Have you enough money?"

"Yes."

At the door the grandmother turned, uncertain.

"Well, then," she said. "You'll wait till tomorrow morning."

"No. I'll go when I have this bag packed. Katharine can send the other things later."

As soon as she was alone again, Anastasia felt a sudden surge of anger that left her shaking with spite. Oh, shame on her! she thought. Shame on her! I have no one to stand up for me.

Tears of self-pity started to her eyes.

Off I go . . .

The suitcase was hard to manage. Katharine came rushing up the stairs to meet her and help her. Katharine was crying but saying nothing.

She bade her grandmother goodbye, where she had come out to stand watching by the sitting-room door, near the hat stand and the hall chair. The grandmother pressed her arm as they kissed, and thrust an envelope of money into her hand.

"Here," she whispered. "God bless you."

She looked strange, senile with emotion, with some distress. Anastasia was full of tears, so that her face pained with the effort of holding them. Katharine had the suitcase. There was a taxicab waiting, and Katharine placed the bag in, clumsily, and closed the door and bent her face to the window. Her face was streaming with tears, and anguished. She had her apron on and the cuffs of her dress were rolled back.

"Goodbye, pet, goodbye. God bless you and keep you. Goodbye, now. Goodbye."

Anastasia nodded wonderingly at her and drove off.

The driver said, "Station?"

"No. The Murray Hotel."

"Oh, I guessed it was to the station you were going," he said mildly.

It was a five-minute drive to the hotel. She used the time to think things through, the clerk and what she would say to him. The driver carried her bag inside and she paid him. She went to the front desk.

"Is Mrs. Dolores Kinsella here?" she asked.

The clerk foraged around at the books in front of him.

"No Kinsella at all here, Miss."

"Oh, dear," she said in humorous distress. "I'll wait for her then. She said she'd be here about this time."

She sat down and looked around her. It was pleasant to rest. She thought of how she had allowed herself to be thrust from her house without a single protest, without one angry word. How easy she had made it for them. She thought, I am not very clever. People can get away with anything.

She had been sitting about ten minutes when she got up and approached the clerk again. He turned to her with a smile.

"She seems to be very late," said Anastasia. "I was going on the mail boat with her."

He glanced efficiently at the clock.

"You have plenty of time. You can catch the late train."

"We were supposed to meet some friends. We thought we'd go on an early train," said Anastasia worriedly.

Now he grew concerned.

"That leaves you very little time. But I'm sure she'll be along soon."

She nodded at her suitcase.

"Will you watch that for me? I have an errand to do, and if Mrs. Kinsella isn't back by the time I return, I'll go on without her. I won't be long."

He nodded in satisfaction at her decision.

She walked composedly out into the street and turned in the direction of Noon Square. She walked without haste. She thought ahead, methodically, to the station, and the boat train, and the boat. Continuing to walk, she opened her purse and searched for the keys to the Paris flat. They were all there, along with the key to her grandmother's house. Everything was in order. She cleared her throat a couple of times.

She walked more slowly as she came to the house, examining it as one might examine a house that had been shuttered for a long time. The steps going up like that to the front door made her sick with longing, to run quick up, and in, and up to her own room with its own view of the meager, dreaming garden.

It was time for tea, once more, the last time. One of the sitting-room windows was wide open. She stared eagerly up at the black open window and immediately was filled with fear that they would close it first. She fancied she heard a noise up there, and thought of them talking unsuspectingly, Mrs. King sitting, Katharine standing, the two of them lost in lifeless discussion, perhaps talking of her by the fire. Comfortable and quiet they are, if sad. How little they know what they will do.

Now then, the square was as busy as ever it was. There were strollers around and in the park, and a noisy knot of errand boys arguing among themselves on the corner. She turned away from them all with a wispy, frightened smile and took her purse and her hat and her gloves and put them down on the path in front of her, and took off her high-heeled shoes and put them with the pile, and leaning awkwardly against the lamp post, pulled off her stockings and tucked them carefully into her shoes.

She stepped back barefooted into the street with her eyes turned expectantly up to the open window. Full of derision and fright, watching where their faces would appear she stared up and began to sing, sudden and loud as one in a dream, who without warning finds a voice in some public place:

"There is a happy land
Far far away
Where we have eggs and ham
Three times a day
Oh it's a happy land
Yes it is . . . "

She was sure of all the words. It was a song she had learned by heart one time, at school. The rowdy errand boys became instantly silent, and so did all the place around, and a passing motorist came to a halt, for a look.

Then there were the two faces, both of them at the window, looking out at her and waving as though they were the ones sailing away, while she called up to them. "Goodbye, Grandmother. Goodbye, Katharine. You see, I haven't gone yet . . ."

EDITOR'S NOTE

Saul Bellow once said that most writers come howling into the world, blind and bare. A few, a handful in every generation, arrive with nails, hair, and teeth, and with eyes that see everything. They speak clearly and coherently, and immediately take up fork and knife at the grownups' table.

The late Maeve Brennan was one of the few. A native Dubliner and a longtime member of the staff of *The New Yorker,* she published her first short story in 1950, when she was thirty-four. "The Holy Terror" was not an apprentice piece; it was the early work of a mature writer, one already in full command of her style and signature subject matter. It tells the story of Mary Ramsay, the ladies' room lady in the Royal Hotel in Dublin, who for thirty years kept a tireless, sour vigil from "a shabby, low-seated bamboo chair set in beside a screen in the corner of the outer room." "She was all eyes and ears." "She took a merciless pleasure in watching women as they passed before her in their most female and desperate and comical predicaments." "Her dislike of these women possessed her completely." "She bore in her heart a long, directionless grudge, a ravenous grudge."

Mary Ramsay, or rather the spirit that animates her, recurs in a number of Maeve's other stories. It is there in Mary Lambert, who in "A Young Girl Can Spoil Her Chances" attempts to "talk sense" to her daughter's suitor, to discourage him from marrying the foolish child who has so often embarrassed her and who now enrages her with the prospect of leaving home. It is there too in Min Bagot, who in "The Springs of Affection" takes revenge on her beautiful, despised sister-in-law by surviving her and appropriating her many fine things.

And it is there in Mrs. King, the grandmother in *The Visitor.* This novella, recently discovered in a university archive and published here for the first time, is the earliest of all of Maeve's known writings. It is also the most representative. It is the ideal place for one to begin with her work, for not only does it show where she set out from but it also explores so much of her later fictional world in small compass. The completeness of vision of *The Visitor,* and the ease with which the novella takes its place among her finest stories, is astonishing. This ferocious tale of love longed for, of love perverted and denied, is one of her finest achievements.

Mrs. King is an embodiment of one side of the Irish temperament, the selfish, emotionally unreachable side. She takes great satisfaction in bringing pain to those who would come between her and her happiness, and her happiness lies in the total possession of her son. There is little natural affection in her, and even less compassion. Her motive force is contempt, especially for those who think her capable of softheartedness.

Mrs. King smiles, but only in anger. Her granddaughter, Anastasia, craves nothing so much from her as a smile of kindness, of approval. This troubled young woman is another of Maeve's archetypes. There is something of her in Delia Bagot, a woman who features in so many of Maeve's best stories, another unloved soul whose neediness drives her toward madness, another motherless daughter who sometimes sees ghosts. There is even more of her in the long-winded lady, the "I" of Maeve's first-person sketches for *The New Yorker*'s Talk of the Town. The long-winded lady is the Flying Dutchman of Manhattan, an exile from a lovingly remembered past, doomed to roam the city with no real home of her own. She is a sad, self-conscious, but exquisite observer, a traveler in residence, a visitor to this life.

In the music of Maeve Brennan, three notes repeatedly sound together—a ravenous grudge, a ravenous nostalgia, and a ravenous need for love. In *The Visitor* she plays this chord for the first time, announcing the key of all the songs to follow.

It is not known exactly when Maeve began to write *The Visitor,* but she completed it sometime in the middle 1940s, when she was living at 5 East Tenth Street, in her adopted Manhattan. If the year is uncertain, the address is not—it is penciled on the cover sheet to the original, an eighty-page, double-spaced, fair-copy typescript.

This typescript—the only extant copy of the work—is now in the Archives of the University of Notre Dame. It came to the library in 1982 as part of its purchase of the business files of Sheed & Ward, the premier Catholic publisher of its day. Maisie Ward, a guiding spirit of the firm, was a well-known figure in the Irish life of mid-century Manhattan, a life that welcomed Maeve upon her coming to the city in 1940. Both women were daughters of illustrious Irishmen—Maisie's father, Wilfrid Ward, was editor of the *Dublin Review;* Maeve's father, Robert Brennan, was the first Irish ambassador to the United States—and it seems that their paths crossed more than once. Maeve probably sent Maisie Ward *The Visitor,* perhaps for possible publication, more likely for general literary advice. All of this is conjecture; exactly how it came to Sheed & Ward is unknown and, according to everyone who knew Maeve, will probably remain so. She was modest, even secretive, about her literary business, and she seldom saved a letter.

I have edited all four of Maeve Brennan's posthumous books. While the others drew on previously published material, most of it from *The New Yorker,* this book marks the first time I've worked on her prose in typescript. I approached it not as a textual scholar but as a trade book editor; that means I cut a repetition here, identified a speaker there, and made a number of small, silent, thrice-considered changes throughout. There were no major cruxes, yet I worried over some of what I did, and still have many questions that I wish I could ask the author, including the very biggest: Why did you never publish this? Was it too short for a first book? Too long for a magazine story? Did you misplace your only carbon of the original? Did you even *make* a carbon? Or did you just move on, having so many stories yet to tell?

William Maxwell, Maeve's editor at *The New Yorker,* told me that she was a shrewd judge of her own prose, never showed him work in progress, and never submitted a story until she could stand by every word of it. I don't know—maybe no one living knows—her own shrewd judgment on *The Visitor.* I can only hope that it was kind, and that she would have stood by this, the published version.

Christopher Carduff
4 August 2000

ABOUT THE AUTHOR

Maeve Brennan left Ireland for America in 1934, when she was seventeen. In 1949 she joined the staff of *The New Yorker,* to which she contributed for more than thirty years. Between 1954 and 1981 she wrote, for The Talk of the Town, a series of sketches about daily life in Manhattan, which she gathered in a book called *The Long-Winded Lady.* Most of her short stories she collected in two volumes, *In and Out of Never-Never Land* and *Christmas Eve;* these and further stories were republished posthumously in *The Springs of Affection* and *The Rose Garden.* Maeve Brennan died in 1993, at the age of seventy-six.